This book belongs to:

_____

HONU AND MOA

written and illustrated by

Edna Cabcabin Moran

BEACHHOUSE

ISBN-10: 1-933067-95-0
ISBN-13: 978-1-933067-95-7
Library of Congress Control Number: 2018949542
Design by Jane Gillespie • Second Printing, August 2019
BeachHouse Publishing, LLC
PO Box 5464 • Kāneʻohe, Hawaiʻi 96744
info@beachhousepublishing.com
www.beachhousepublishing.com

Printed by RRD Shenzhen, China 5/2019

Dedicated with aloha to:

Dominic, Kaleia, Aria Jacen, Jaxon, Alix, Cassius, Caleb, Van, Bryson Jett, Kyleigh, Asher, Mollee, Maddox, Owen, Pearl, and William "Ren."

Honu, the green sea turtle, took a sip from the spring, which was a fine treat after her long swim.

A nearby waterfall tinkled like bells, inspiring Honu to sing in a smooth, clear voice:

Trickle, trickle little stream
flowing from my lovely spring…

"BWAAAHK!! No, no!" A giant bird burst through a cluster of trees. It was Moa, the rooster. He screeched, "It is NOT your spring. You can't say that!"

Honu said, "Well, I just did."

Moa puffed his feathers. "This is MY spring!" He scratched at the ground and let out a SQUAWWWWK! followed by a rant of reasons why he owned the spring. "I have been coming here since I was a little fluffy thing!" he said.

Honu shook her head. "I still do not think it is your spring." She stared at Moa for a long time without blinking.

Moa puffed his chest and said, "Well, Honu, you're just plain wrong! But I don't have all day to argue. We should settle our disagreement."

Honu tilted her head. "What exactly do you mean?"

"Why don't we compete for this place? Let's return to our homes on the other side of the island,"continued Moa. "You go back to the shore, and I will go home to the forest. Then, tomorrow morning, we'll race back, and whoever gets here first may claim it for himself!"

Honu sat, thinking.

Finally, she said, "How do I know you will be fair? Who will watch over our contest?"

Moa paced and scratched at the ground. Finally, he said, "Let's ask Sun to awaken us. He is wise and can watch us from the sky!"

Honu replied, "I will agree on one condition. Whoever wins keeps the spring not only for herself, but also for her 'ohana and future generations."

Moa took a deep breath and thought, "That will be a much better prize for me."

"Agreed," said Moa.

Later that day, Honu and Moa asked Sun to judge their race. Sun shone down on them and agreed with a nod.

Moa and Honu journeyed back to their homes and settled down for the night.

The next morning, Sun brought forth
the early light of dawn, waking Honu.

Honu slipped into the mouth of a cold, bubbling
stream. Its waters flowed in the opposite direction of
her travels. Honu swam with all her might, pushing her
legs against the current. She rested on mossy boulders
along the way. But, most of all, she swam.

Moa was also awakened by Sun. Cackling at the thought of Honu losing the contest, Moa thought, "Why should I bother leaving early? Honu is slow!" Moa went back to sleep.

Once again, he was awakened, but this time by sprinkles of rain. Squawking frantically, Moa took flight, darting through a thicket of trees. "Make way for me! Make way!" he screeched.

As Moa neared the spring, he thought, "I'm almost there, and I'm surely ahead of Honu, so why rush?"

Moa flew up to the tallest tree branch and watched as Sun beamed a rainbow through the clouds.

Moa teased Sun, saying, "That's nice but I've seen better!"

Then Sun shone a magnificent double rainbow against the clouds.

"You think you're fancy? SQUAWK!
Look at ME…!"

Moa flew above the trees and displayed a brilliant
cape of feathers. He put on a fantastic show, changing the
colors of his cape in any way he pleased. Moa
squawked with pride long after Sun's double
rainbow faded.

Then Moa remembered he had a contest to win. Hastily, he flew down and landed on a branch above the spring. From there, he heard a light, playful song:

Trickle, trickle, little stream,
flowing from my lovely spring.
'Tis an honor and a dream
to win a most important thing!"

There was Honu, in the middle of the spring.

Sun shone down on Honu, who waved in greeting.

Moa scratched at the tree branch and muttered, "Ho'omaika'i…Congratulations."

"Mahalo," said Honu. "I am the winner, but I am also fair. Your 'ohana may use the spring…"

"…but NOT you," added Honu.

"Huh? Why can't I?!" asked Moa.

"You LOST!" said Honu.

Moa was squawkless.

Honu chuckled and said, "Moa, you can visit the spring as well. No one can claim the spring for herself, for it belongs to everyone!"

"Says who?" asked Moa.

"Says one who is bright and wise and knows how to keep a foolish bird busy!" Honu gazed up, winked at Sun, and dove into the sparkling water.

Author's Note

Honu and Moa, a Hawaiiana retelling of Aesop's fable *The Tortoise and the Hare*, is loosely based on the research of renowned Hawaiian historian Kumu Mary Kawena Pukui, and other scholars whose volumes of myths feature kupua, or supernatural beings.

Honu's character reflects a deep respect for ʻohana (family) and the delicate ecosystems and resources of Hawaiʻi—notably its sacred, fresh spring ponds and tributaries carrying distinct names, such as nuku muliwai, which refers to a stream that meets the sea. This type of waterway challenges Honu as she swims upstream, back to the poʻowai, the source of spring waters. (Please note that the book's illustrations are imagined places and do not depict actual sites in Hawaiʻi.)

I was inspired by Kumu Kawena's story of the kupua green sea turtles who arrive at Punaluʻu—a mother turtle named Honupoʻokea and a father turtle called Honuʻea. Both dig into the earth and create a spring for their daughter hatchling, Kauila, whose colors resemble the polished wood of the kauila tree.

Another Hawaiian story tells of two kupua roosters, Kaʻauhelemoa and Lepeʻamoa, whose epic and colorful sky battle is alluded to in Moa's lofty display of pride toward the Sun. Early versions of this tale may be found in W.D. Westervelt's book, *Legends of Old Honolulu*, and in the kāhiko hula *Pā Ka Makani*.

Sources

Beckwith, Martha Warren. *Hawaiian Mythology*. New Haven: Yale University Press, 1940.

Handy, E.S., E.G. Handy, Mary Kawena Pukui. *Native Planters in Old Hawaii: Their Life, Lore, and Environment*, Issue 233. Honolulu: Bishop Museum Press, 1972.

Westervelt, W. D., *Hawaiian Legends of Old Honolulu*. Boston: Press of Geo. H. Ellis Co., 1915.

Kamakau, Samuel M. *Works of the People of Old*. Honolulu: Bishop Museum Press, 1976.

Acknowledgments

Mahalo nui loa to: Kumu Patrick Makuakāne and Hālau Nā Lei Hulu I Ka Wēkiu for their depth of aloha, knowledge, and inspiration; author and hula sis, Connie Hale, members of the Prose Shop, especially Laura Wynkoop, the Perfictionists critique group, fellow teaching artist and friend, Jenna Freck, and fellow Killer Rabbits, Laura Elliot and Dee White for the invaluable feedback and support; my hoaloha, scholar Teri Skillman and my wonderful publisher, Jane Gillespie, for their akamai feedback and leads to key visual references of the natural ponds and springs of Oʻahu; and my loving ʻohana and beta readers, Mark, Kailani, and Luke, for "everything."